RUPERT

and the Emperor's Gong

EXPRESS NEWSPAPERS plc, Ludgate House,
245 Blackfriars Road,
London SE1 9UX.

Produced by Brainwaves Limited
5 Highwood Ridge, Hatch Warren, Basingstoke,
Hampshire RG22 4UU.

ISBN 0–85079–252–5

Printed and bound in Singapore.

'What are we going to get Ping-Pong for his birthday tomorrow?' sighs Bill. 'It would be nice to find him something Chinese to remind him of home.' 'Why don't we go down to the old antique shop in the village,' suggests Rupert. 'We're bound to see something he'd like there!'

Soon the two pals are having a great time among all the treasures they find in the shop. 'What about this toy train?' asks Rupert. 'He's got one,' says Bill. Then Rupert spots something interesting under a table. 'Look at this, Bill!' he cries. 'It's a gong, they use them in China to wake people up in the morning!' 'That's perfect,' says Bill, 'all it needs is a good polish!'

Next morning Rupert and Bill hurry over to Pong-Ping's house with their present. 'Happy birthday!' they cry as he opens the box. 'What a wonderful surprise!' beams Pong-Ping.

Then he notices the Chinese writing on the gong. 'This is royal property!' he exclaims. 'It belongs to a great Emperor and must be returned without delay!' 'How are we going to do that?' asks Rupert. 'Come with me,' says Pong-Ping, leading his pals to a small building in his garden. 'It's lucky I have a lift to China, he says, 'we must go there to find the gong's owner!'

As soon as they arrive in China, Pong-Ping takes Rupert and Bill to meet his wise old friend, Li-Poo. 'A-ha!' says the old man, examining the gong. 'This belongs to the Emperor of the Very Far East!'

'Oh dear!' sighs Pong-Ping. 'That's the other side of the High Mountains, we'll never be able to get there!' 'Let me call the Dragon Master,' smiles Li-Poo, 'he may let you ride there on a dragon!' 'Why, of course!' says the Dragon Master. 'But you must be very careful, something is wrong in the Very Far East, everyone there seems to be very angry!'

The Dragon Master brings his fastest dragon and the three pals climb up on its back. 'Are you sure it's safe?' asks Bill. 'Of course,' laughs the Dragon Master, 'just hold tight!' As soon as the friends are ready, the dragon rises high above the rooftops.

Far below, Rupert can see Li-Poo and the Dragon Master waving goodbye to them. 'To the very Far East!' orders Pong-Ping, and the dragon starts to fly like the wind. 'This is fun!' laughs Bill, as they fly over villages and towns, until the last house has been left far behind.

Soaring high over a ridge of snow-capped mountains, the dragon starts to glide down towards a distant building. 'That must be the Emperor's palace!' cries Rupert. As soon as they land the pals are surrounded by stern-looking soldiers.

'All strangers go to the Grand Vizier!' a guard says gruffly. Leaving the dragon, the chums are taken to the throne room. 'We'd like to see the Emperor,' says Pong-Ping. 'Impossible!' barks the Grand Vizier angrily. 'Take them to the dungeons!'

'You've woken the dragon!' says Bill, and Pong-Ping calls to it for help. The dragon takes a deep breath and shoots out a blast of flame, melting the bars as if they were chocolate. 'Well done,' says Rupert, 'now let's escape!'

Once in their cell, the pals peer through the bars of the window and see the dragon asleep in the courtyard. 'If only we could get out we'd be able to fly home!' sighs Pong-Ping. 'I've an idea!' cries Rupert, banging the gong.

Clambering through the window, the pals are halfway across the courtyard when the Grand Vizier comes running out of the palace. 'Oh no!' gasps Bill, 'we've had it now!' But to Rupert's surprise the Vizier is smiling.

'The Emperor has woken up!' he laughs. 'Woken up?' asks Rupert. 'Yes,' replies the Vizier, 'he's been fast asleep ever since his gong went missing. We've tried everything to wake him, but only the gong will work!' The Grand Vizier then explains how he had to stop anyone finding out what had happened. 'And when you arrived we thought you were spies!' he says. 'No,' smiles Rupert, 'we came to give this gong back!'

When the Emperor learns what has happened, he insists on meeting the three pals. 'Thank you for returning my gong,' he says, and then to the friends' surprise they hear the sound of the gong being struck once more.

'Your feast is ready!' smiles the Emperor, leading them to a huge banquet. When it's over their dragon is summoned and the pals start for home. 'This is the best birthday I've *ever* had!' says Pong-Ping.